Dear Parents and Educators,

Welcome to Penguin Young Readers! As parents and educators, you know that each child develops at his or her own pace—in terms of speech, critical thinking, and, of course, reading. Penguin Young Readers recognizes this fact. As a result, each Penguin Young Readers book is assigned a traditional easy-to-read level (1–4) as well as a Guided Reading Level (A–P). Both of these systems will help you choose the right book for your child. Please refer to the back of each book for specific leveling information. Penguin Young Readers features esteemed authors and illustrators, stories about favorite characters, fascinating nonfiction, and more!

Princess Buttercup
A Flower Princess Story

LEVEL **2**

GUIDED READING LEVEL **E**

This book is perfect for a **Progressing Reader** who:
- can figure out unknown words by using picture and context clues;
- can recognize beginning, middle, and ending sounds;
- can make and confirm predictions about what will happen in the text; and
- can distinguish between fiction and nonfiction.

Here are some **activities** you can do during and after reading this book:
- Problem/Solution: Discuss the problem and solution in the story.
- Character Feelings: Princess Buttercup experiences many things in the story and feels differently during each one. Discuss how she feels during the following scenes:
  - on the first day of spring
  - as she is picking buttercups
  - when she realizes she is lost
  - as she rides on the butterfly
  - when she arrives at the party

Remember, sharing the love of reading with a child is the best gift you can give!

—Bonnie Bader, EdM
   Penguin Young Readers program

*Penguin Young Readers are leveled by independent reviewers applying the standards developed by Irene Fountas and Gay Su Pinnell in *Matching Books to Readers: Using Leveled Books in Guided Reading*, Heinemann, 1999.

For Jane O'Connor,
a constant inspiration—WCL

For Shawn Michael Gordon—JS

Penguin Young Readers
Published by the Penguin Group
Penguin Group (USA) Inc., 375 Hudson Street, New York, New York 10014, USA
Penguin Group (Canada), 90 Eglinton Avenue East, Suite 700, Toronto, Ontario M4P 2Y3, Canada
(a division of Pearson Penguin Canada Inc.)
Penguin Books Ltd., 80 Strand, London WC2R 0RL, England
Penguin Group Ireland, 25 St. Stephen's Green, Dublin 2, Ireland (a division of Penguin Books Ltd.)
Penguin Group (Australia), 250 Camberwell Road, Camberwell, Victoria 3124, Australia
(a division of Pearson Australia Group Pty. Ltd.)
Penguin Books India Pvt. Ltd., 11 Community Centre, Panchsheel Park, New Delhi—110 017, India
Penguin Group (NZ), 67 Apollo Drive, Rosedale, Auckland 0632, New Zealand
(a division of Pearson New Zealand Ltd.)
Penguin Books (South Africa) (Pty.) Ltd., 24 Sturdee Avenue,
Rosebank, Johannesburg 2196, South Africa

Penguin Books Ltd., Registered Offices: 80 Strand, London WC2R 0RL, England

Library of Congress Control Number: 2001277326

ISBN 978-0-448-42472-9   10 9 8 7 6 5 4 3

PENGUIN YOUNG READERS

LEVEL
PROGRESSING
READER
2

Princess Buttercup
A Flower Princess Story

WITHDRAWN

by Wendy Cheyette Lewison
illustrated by Jerry Smath

Penguin Young Readers
An Imprint of Penguin Group (USA) Inc.

In the magic garden,

six Flower Princesses

open their eyes.

Wake up, wake up!

It is the first day of spring!

There is going to be a party.

Princess Lily and Princess Tulip

set the table.

Princess Rose gets

the band ready.

Princess Hyacinth makes a cake.

Princess Iris makes

up a game to play

at the party.

But where is Princess Buttercup?

7

Princess Buttercup is
out picking buttercups.
One buttercup here.
Two buttercups there.
Now she has lots of
buttercups for the party.

8

Look!

It is a butterfly.

"How pretty!" she says.

She follows the butterfly.

She forgets all about

the buttercups.

She forgets all about the party.

The butterfly hops

from flower to flower.

Princess Buttercup skips after it.

She looks around.

Where is the butterfly?

And where is she?

Oh no!

She is in the woods.

And she is lost.

But the butterfly is not lost.

It is still looking for flowers.

Princess Buttercup has an idea.

She holds up a buttercup.

Then she sings this song:

Butterfly, butterfly,

bright as can be.

Fly, pretty butterfly,

fly down to me!

Soon the butterfly sees

the buttercup.

Down, down it flies.

Now the butterfly is just

over her head.

She grabs hold of it and . . .

Whee!

Off they go!

22

24

At last,

there is the magic garden.

Princess Buttercup is not

lost anymore.

Down, down comes
Princess Buttercup
on the butterfly.

27

Plop!

The butterfly lands

on a flower.

Princess Buttercup

climbs down.

The Flower Princesses are

happy to see her.

And she is happy to see them.

The party begins.

Everybody has fun.

Even the butterfly!